D0448790

A NOTE TO PARENTS

When your children are ready to "step into reading," giving them the right books—and lots of them—is as crucial as giving them the right food to eat. **Step into Reading Books** present exciting stories and information reinforced with lively, colorful illustrations that make learning to read fun, satisfying, and worthwhile. They are priced so that acquiring an entire library of them is affordable. And they are beginning readers with an important difference— they're written on four levels.

Step 1 Books, with their very large type and extremely simple vocabulary, have been created for the very youngest readers. **Step 2 Books** are both longer and slightly more difficult. **Step 3 Books,** written to mid-second-grade reading levels, are for the child who has acquired even greater reading skills. **Step 4 Books** offer exciting nonfiction for the increasingly proficient reader.

Children develop at different ages. **Step into Reading Books,** with their four levels of reading, are designed to help children become good—and interested—readers *faster*. The grade levels assigned to the four steps—preschool through grade 1 for Step 1, grades 1 through 3 for Step 2, grades 2 and 3 for Step 3, and grades 2 through 4 for Step 4—are intended only as guides. Some children move through all four steps very rapidly; others climb the steps over a period of several years. These books will help your child "step into reading" in style!

To my editor, Mallory Loehr,
who never insists, is usually right, and is always there
                                        —J. S.

And with thanks to Miss Pearl—
wherever she is—
for letting me illustrate my fourth-grade reports
                                        —T. S.

Text copyright © 1995 by Janice Shefelman. Illustrations copyright © 1995 by
Tom Shefelman. All rights reserved under International and Pan-American Copyright Conventions.
Published in the United States by Random House, Inc., New York, and simultaneously in Canada by
Random House of Canada Limited, Toronto.

Library of Congress Cataloging-in-Publication Data:
Shefelman, Janice Jordan. Young Wolf's First Hunt / by Janice Shefelman ;
illustrated by Tom Shefelman. p. cm.—(Step into reading. A step 3 book)
SUMMARY: Although his father thinks that Young Wolf is still too young to join in
the tribe's buffalo hunt, the ten-year-old tries to prepare himself, his horse, and a
friend to take part.
ISBN 0-679-86364-8 (trade) — ISBN 0-679-96364-2 (lib. bdg.)
[1. Indians of North America—Juvenile fiction. 2. Bison—Fiction.]
I. Shefelman, Tom, ill. II. Title. III. Series: Step into reading. Step 3 book.
PZ7.S54115 Yo 1994 [E]—dc20 94-9530

Manufactured in the United States of America   10 9 8 7 6 5 4 3 2 1

STEP INTO READING is a trademark of Random House, Inc.

Step into Reading

Young Wolf's First Hunt

By Janice Shefelman
Illustrated by Tom Shefelman

A Step 3 Book

Random House New York

1
A Secret

Young Wolf ran to keep up with his father.

"I see that you have learned how to use your bow," said Eagle Feather. "Your mother will be pleased by the meat we bring her."

Young Wolf's heart swelled. Now maybe Father will let me run buffalo, he thought.

It would soon be time for the buffalo hunt. Everyone in the village needed warm robes and meat for the winter.

That night Young Wolf said, "Father, I think I am ready to run buffalo. And kill a calf."

Eagle Feather smiled. "You have a strong arm and a sharp eye. But you are too young, my son. Running buffalo is dangerous. And Red Wind is not a buffalo horse."

"I can teach her," said Young Wolf.

Eagle Feather shook his head. "No, you are too young." He looked at Young Wolf's mother.

Voice of the Sunrise nodded. "Wait until you are eleven, my son—only one more winter."

"Grandfather could help me," said Young Wolf.

Eagle Feather looked hard at him. "I have spoken. You are too young."

Too young, too young, too young!
thought Young Wolf.

He stood up. "I wish my name was
Old Wolf," he said. Then he ducked out
the opening.

Red Wind was beside the tepee.

"Father says I am too young," whispered Young Wolf. "And you are not a buffalo horse."

Young Wolf wanted people in the village to say, "Young Wolf has killed his first buffalo. Soon he will be a man."

Red Wind nuzzled his ear.

"Are you trying to tell me a secret?" Young Wolf asked. He stroked her forehead. Suddenly, he knew the secret.

"You want to learn to run buffalo! So Father will change his mind."

2
Discovered

In the morning Young Wolf rode across the creek and over a hill.

"No one will see us here," he said.

Then he tied a long rope to Red Wind's lower jaw, as the warriors did.

"First you must learn to run without stepping on this rope," he told her. "It will drag behind you. So if I fall off, I can grab it."

Young Wolf did not think Red Wind would run away from him. But what if a buffalo charged her...with his huge head down...and his sharp horns pointed at her side? What would Red Wind do then?

For days they practiced. Young Wolf
ran while Red Wind trotted beside him.
Time after time she stepped on the rope
and fell.

"Like this, Red Wind." Young Wolf
lifted his feet high.

Red Wind watched him. She began to
prance and dance.

"Yes!" said Young Wolf.

One day he saw Little Big Mouth and
his horse, Shadow.

"Oh, no," Young Wolf whispered.

"Hey, Baby Wolf! Are you teaching your mare to run?" Little Big Mouth yelled.

Young Wolf clenched his fists. But he remembered Grandfather He-Bear's words. *It is not manly to fight among ourselves.*

More than anything Young Wolf wanted to be a man.

Then Young Wolf had a good idea. Little Big Mouth and his horse could help.

"Come down here," Young Wolf called. "And I'll tell you something."

Little Big Mouth came. "What?" he asked.

Young Wolf folded his arms. "We could train our horses to run buffalo."

Little Big Mouth's big mouth opened. "I thought your father said no."

"He did," Young Wolf said.

"So did mine." Little Big Mouth kicked at the dirt.

"Maybe we could change their minds," said Young Wolf.

Little Big Mouth looked up.

"We could teach our horses to turn away at the sound of a bowstring," Young Wolf went on. "So they won't be gored if a wounded buffalo charges."

Slowly Little Big Mouth smiled.

Side by side they galloped across the
meadow. Little Big Mouth pulled his
bowstring back. *Twang!* He nudged
Shadow with his knee. The horse turned
away from Red Wind.

"Now you," said Little Big Mouth.

Day after day the two boys practiced.
Finally both horses learned to turn away
without even a nudge. And Shadow
learned to run with the rope dragging
under his hooves.

One afternoon they saw Eagle Feather
on the hill.

"Uh-oh," said Little Big Mouth.

Eagle Feather turned and rode away.

"Is he angry?" Little Big Mouth asked.

"I don't know," said Young Wolf.

After supper Eagle Feather said,
"Come, my son. We will talk under the
stars. Bring fire to light my pipe."

Young Wolf followed him out into the
night. What would Father say?

"I have watched you for many days,"
he began. "I saw that you taught Red Wind
to run buffalo. Even though I forbade it."

"Yes, Father."

"That did not please me," said
Eagle Feather. "But I saw something else.
Something that made me proud."

"Proud, Father?"

"Yes. I saw that you acted like a man.
That you and Little Big Mouth worked
together."

Eagle Feather blew smoke to the sky.
Young Wolf's heart rose with it.

"So, I have changed my mind. You may
run buffalo with me, my son. We will see
what you can do."

3
Buffalo Fear

The new moon rose—the moon of frosted grass. A fire was lit in the middle of the village. Drummers began to beat their drums.

Young Wolf danced around the fire with the warriors. They sang a song to the buffalo spirit.

"Oh, mighty buffalo,
Listen to my plea.
Oh, mighty buffalo,
Give yourself to me."

Then Eagle Feather held up his hand for quiet. "Who would tell his story?"

White Rabbit arose. He was an old man with a lame leg.

"Once I ran buffalo," he began. "I let my arrow fly. It passed through one buffalo and into another—two with one arrow!"

"Yip, yip, yip!" people shouted.

White Rabbit pulled up his legging. He showed a long white scar. "Here a buffalo left his hunting picture on my leg."

Young Wolf felt a stab of fear. He began to think about pointed horns and hunting pictures.

At dawn the hunting party started off.
Eagle Feather and the other men rode at
the front. Women and children brought up
the rear. In between, Young Wolf rode
beside Little Big Mouth.

"Well, your idea worked, Young Wolf,"
said Little Big Mouth. "Our first buffalo
run. Are you afraid?"

Young Wolf shook his head. He no
longer hated Little Big Mouth. He even
liked him—a little. But not enough to tell
him the truth.

"Are you?" Young Wolf asked.

"Me?" Little Big Mouth said. "Nothing scares me."

Young Wolf's heart lay on the ground. How could he become a man if he was afraid?

Finally they came to a valley. It was black with grazing buffalo, like a dark lake stirred by the wind.

"We will camp here," Eagle Feather said.

When night came, Young Wolf crawled under his robe and fell asleep.

And he dreamed.

The herd of buffalo came thundering out of the valley, heading straight for him. Young Wolf leaped onto Red Wind's back. "Run," he yelled. But her legs were like tree trunks. The buffalo came closer and closer. A bull lowered his huge head. His horns were pointed at Red Wind…

"Wake up, Young Wolf," called Eagle Feather. "It is time to run buffalo."

Young Wolf got up. He could still hear the pounding hooves in his ears.

Voice of the Sunrise handed him a piece of dried meat. "Eat," she told him. "You will need your strength."

Young Wolf took a small bite. But his throat seemed to close. He chewed and chewed.

"Remember," Eagle Feather said. "You must ride close to the buffalo—close enough to feel his heat. That is the only way to make a kill."

Young Wolf nodded and swallowed the bite. His stomach tied a knot around it.

4
Buffalo Run

Young Wolf rode at his father's side.
The north wind blew in his face, and he
shivered. Red Wind sniffed the air.

Young Wolf looked to the right and left—until he found Little Big Mouth. Was he afraid now?

The buffalo did not see them. Or hear them. Or smell them. The calves were in the center, protected by the big buffalo.

Eagle Feather leaned close. "When I give the sign, we will go among the calves."

Young Wolf caught his breath. That meant riding through the big buffalo— with their sharp horns!

A bull lifted his head and snorted. He struck the ground with his hoof. *Thump, thump, thump.* The herd began to run.

When Eagle Feather raised his bow, the warriors broke into a gallop.

Young Wolf and his father caught up to the herd. It was like following thunder across the sky. Oh, why had he begged to come?

Eagle Feather rode into the herd.
Young Wolf followed in his wake. All
around him buffalo crowded together.
Their horns clacked. Young Wolf's heart
pounded against his ribs.

He looked over at Little Big Mouth. His
eyes were wide. He is afraid too, thought
Young Wolf. He put his fist on his chest.
"Strong heart!" he yelled.

Little Big Mouth made the same sign.

Eagle Feather pointed to a calf.

Young Wolf leaned forward. Red Wind stretched out her legs and chased the calf.

"Closer," Eagle Feather shouted.

Young Wolf nudged her closer. He set an arrow and pulled the bowstring back.

Then he heard bellowing behind him. It was a cow. Was she the calf's mother?

Hurry and shoot, thought Young Wolf. Quickly he aimed at the soft spot behind the ribs. *Twang!*

Red Wind turned away. But the arrow flew over the calf's head.

Again Young Wolf moved close. So close he could feel the calf's heat.

"Shoot, shoot!" shouted Eagle Feather.

Young Wolf drew the arrow and aimed carefully. *Twang!*

It plunged deep into the calf's side— all the way to the fcathers.

As Red Wind turned, Young Wolf looked back.

The calf staggered and fell.

Now the cow charged Young Wolf. Her horns pointed at Red Wind's side.

"No!" Young Wolf grabbed Red Wind's mane and pulled. She reared up.

The cow ran under Red Wind's hooves! Red Wind spun around on her hind legs.

Young Wolf's head whirled. He felt himself slipping…Suddenly the ground hit him. It knocked the breath out of his body.

More buffalo were coming! Their thunder filled the air. Even if he could call his mare, would she hear him?

Red Wind tossed her head. The rope flew from side to side. But she did not run.

When the rope landed near Young Wolf, he grabbed it. He gave a tug.

"Nnnnn-hhhhh," she said, and came to him.

Young Wolf climbed on and clung to her mane. Red Wind bolted out of the path of the herd.

As soon as the herd had passed,
Eagle Feather rode up beside his son.
"Red Wind is a fine buffalo horse," he said.
"And she has a brave hunter on her back."
    Young Wolf was still out of breath.
"Did you see...how she stayed with me?"
    "I saw, my son. And I saw how you
killed a calf."

Eagle Feather motioned Young Wolf to
follow. "It is time to give thanks."

They rode back to the center of the
valley, where Young Wolf's calf lay.
Nearby, Little Big Mouth stood over the
calf he had killed.

Young Wolf dismounted and lifted his
arms.

> "Oh, sacred buffalo,
> You gave your life to me.
> For that I give you thanks,
> And set your spirit free."

5
Friends

At the feast Eagle Feather stood to speak.

"Our two youngest hunters killed their first buffalo—Little Big Mouth and my son. Their tepees will never lack for meat." He motioned to High Horse.

Little Big Mouth's father stood. "My son makes my heart glad. So I will give a robe to Medicine Woman, who has no hunter."

She nodded her thanks.

Then it was Eagle Feather's turn.

"To show my pleasure, I will give a fine horse to White Rabbit, who has none."

The old man grinned. "It is a generous thing you do, Eagle Feather. I will sing of Young Wolf's first hunt for moons to come," he said.

Grandfather He-Bear leaned close to Young Wolf. "Tell me, Grandson, were you afraid?"

Young Wolf looked down. "Yes, Grandfather."

His grandfather smiled. "You are closer to being a man now. Do you know why?"

"Because I killed a calf?" Young Wolf asked.

"No, because you did what you were afraid to do."

Young Wolf's heart soared. If
Grandfather He-Bear said so, it must be
true. For he was very old and wise.

Later Young Wolf looked everywhere
for Little Big Mouth. He found him sitting
on a rocky ledge.

"Were you afraid?" asked Young Wolf.

Little Big Mouth was silent. Then he said, "Were *you?*"

"Can you keep a secret?" Young Wolf asked.

Little Big Mouth nodded.

"Yes, I was," said Young Wolf.

"So was I," said Little Big Mouth.

Young Wolf looked at him. "But if you do what you are afraid to do, you become a man."

Little Big Mouth grinned. "And if you tell someone a secret, you become his friend."

"Yes." Young Wolf smiled. "Friends."